For little Ugo

My thanks to Francine

First American Edition published in 2006 by Enchanted Lion Books, 45 Main Street, Suite 519, Brooklyn, NY 11201

Originally published in French as *Le Cheval magique de Han Gan* by l'école des loisirs © 2004
Translation © 2006 Enchanted Lion Books

For information about permissions to reproduce selections from this book, write to:
Permissions, Enchanted Lion Books, 45 Main Street, Suite 519, Brooklyn, NY 11201

[A CIP record is on file with the Library of Congress]

ISBN 1-59270-063-2

Printed in China

2 4 6 8 10 9 7 5 3 1

CHEN JIANG HONG

The Magic Horse
of Han Gan

Translated by Claudia Zoe Bedrick

ENCHANTED LION BOOKS
New York

When he was little, Han Gan loved to draw.

But he was unable to buy brushes and paper because his family was too poor.

To help his parents by earning a little money, he went to work for the innkeeper.

His job was to deliver meals to the homes of her customers.

One day, Han Gan delivered a meal
to the famous painter Wang Wei.

As he was leaving, he noticed some handsome horses behind the house

and could not resist sketching them in the sand.

Intrigued, Wang Wei drew up behind Han Gan and looked thoughtfully at his drawing.

Then he told Han Gan to come back and see him the following day.

Han Gan returned the next day to find that Wang Wei had prepared paper,
ink, brushes and a small sac of coins for him.
"This is for you, so that you can paint as much as you like."
Han Gan's heart swelled with this recognition.

Han Gan drew from sunrise to sunset.
More than anything, he loved to draw horses, always trying
to make them seem as real and alive as possible.

He was so talented that several years later,
the Emperor, who had heard a great deal about him,
summoned him to the palace to enter the
Academy for official painters.

At the Academy, Han Gan refused to perfect his craft by imitating the works
of the ancient masters, as his teacher asked him to do.
He only wanted to paint horses, which, strangely enough, he always painted tethered.
"Why do you always draw your horses hitched-up?" his friends asked him one day.
"Because," Han Gan replied, "my horses are so alive they might leap right off the paper."

From this time on, people began to whisper ever-stranger things about the horses of Han Gan.

Some time later, in the deepest darkness of a silent night,

a great warrior came to see Han Gan as he worked in his studio.

"My visit must remain secret," the warrior said. "The enemy is at our gates. Tomorrow, I must go and fight."

"I have heard that your horses
are more real than nature and that
your magic brush can make them come
to life. If I asked you, could you bring to
life a steed more valiant and spirited
than has ever before existed?"
"I can try," Han Gan replied.

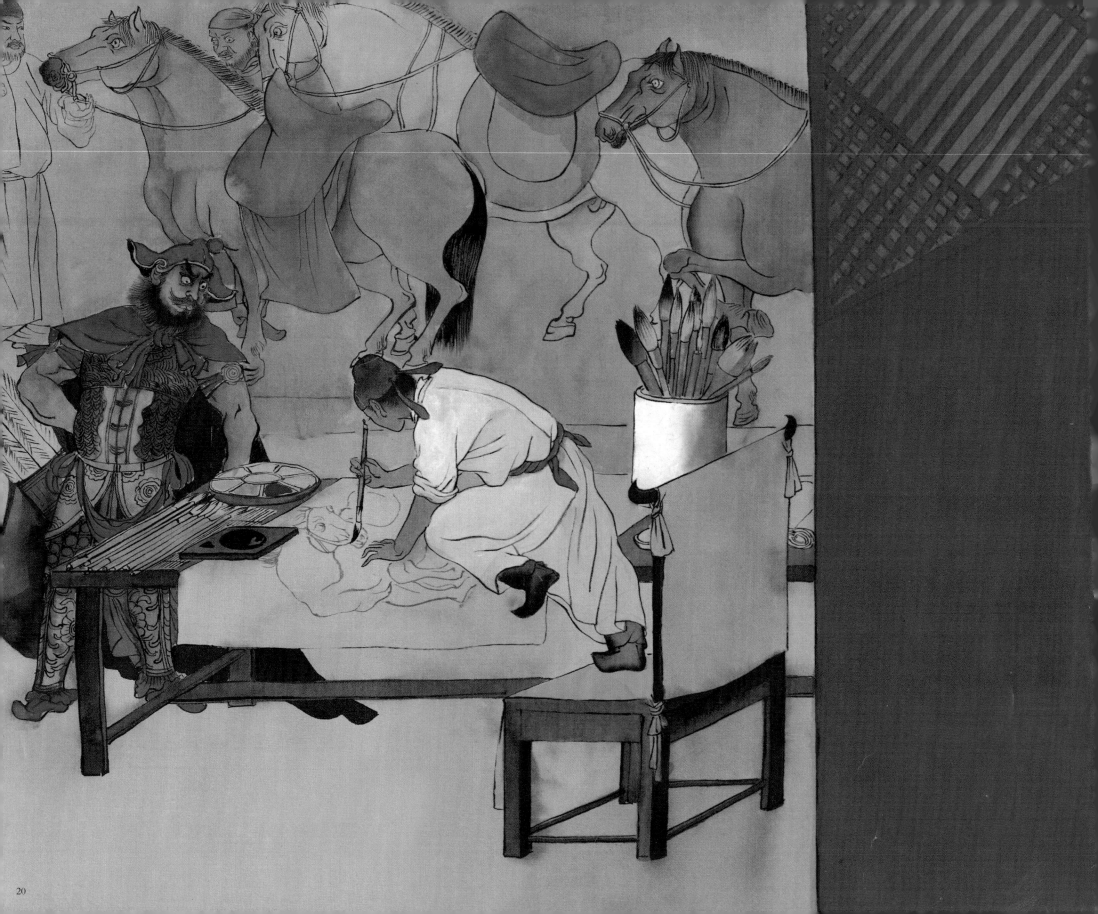

Han Gan started to draw with all his
heart and soul, but the horse that he
created did not come to life.
"Please carry on. It is crucial,"
the warrior insisted.
"I am sorry," said Han Gan.
"This drawing is worthless. It
deserves only to be thrown
into the fire."

But at the very moment
that he threw away the
paper, an extraordinary
steed bounded out from
between the flames.

The warrior hurled himself onto his mount and
disappeared with him into the night.
"Take care of your horse!" Han Gan called after him.
But only the moon was there to hear him.

The horse that had come to life   had no need of water, food, or sleep.

When he galloped, his hooves
barely touched the ground.

As for the warrior, he
had never felt so mighty.

And he was not simply powerful. He seemed invincible.
In the fiercest battles, neither the arrows nor the spears ever touched him.
Not him or his horse. The warrior began to report great victories.

But these victories did not satisfy him.
He wanted to fight again and again until he no longer had a single living enemy.
Sadness overcame the horse. He looked around at the defeated and the dead
and at the wounded and dying horses, and suddenly he began to cry.

Throwing off the warrior in the middle of the battlefield,
the horse, still covered in blood, broke into a powerful gallop.
Nothing and no one could have stopped him.

The warrior searched desperately for the horse.
He searched for him over thirty-six days and through thirty-six nights.
One autumn morning, he arrived in front of Han Gan's house.

"The horse that you gave me has disappeared," he said to Han Gan. "Do you know where he is?"
"Yes, I do," Han Gan replied. "Do you see this painting? In it, I painted five horses. One morning when I arose,
I found a sixth. It is here in my painting that your horse now lives."

Horses and Grooms, Han Gan, ink and pigment on silk, the Cernuschi Museum, Paris. © Photo Archives of the Museums of the City of Paris

The magic horse is a legend, but Han Gan really existed.
He lived in China 1,200 years ago and was an extraordinary painter
of horses. His paintings inspire the imagination, and although only a few
have survived the passage of time, nevertheless Han Gan has continued to
be recognized as a great painter.

Chen Jiang Hong painted the illustrations for this book directly on silk
using the same technique as that employed by Han Gan.